Patches the Beaver

Welcome to Harmony Woods

Story by Shane Gauthier
Illustrated by Gabriel Wong

Copyright © 2007 Harmony Woods Press Inc.

All rights reserved. No part of this book may be reproduced or utilized in any form or by any means, electronic or mechanical, including photocopying, recording, or any information storage and retrieval system without permission in writing from the publisher.

Published in Canada by Harmony Woods Press Inc., Edmonton, Alberta.

Library of Congress Cataloging in Publication Data is available.

A CIP catalogue record for this book is available from the British Library.

ISBN 1-55858-632-6 (trade binding) 10 9 8 7 6 5 4 3 2 1

ISBN 1-55858-632-6 (library binding) 10 9 8 7 6 5 4 3 2 1

For more information about the book, author, or illustrator, please visit **www.patchesthebeaver.com**

Author's Note

Jeff, thank you for your valuable feedback and sharp eyes that brought this book to the next level.

This book symbolizes Shane's commitment to promoting the rich diversity that exists in our world's communities. This is Shane's first children's book.

It is a bright and warm fall day in Harmony Woods. There is a brilliant blue sky, completely clear, except for one dark cloud on the horizon.

Hopping along, Lucky Rabbit hurries home with tremendous excitement after eating his favorite carrot soup, crisp lily pad salad, and beet juice at the Hippity Hop Diner. Hippity hop, hippity hop, he jumps down the hill.

With one great big

hippity hop,

Lucky rockets into the air with such
speed that he catapults himself...

... into Chew Chew Bubblegum Factory's pond.

Staggering out of the pond disoriented, Lucky cleans the bubblegum from his glasses and begins to gather his scattered books.

He spots his friends Feather Goose, Star Squirrel, Duke of Cannot, the Toad, and Speedy Tortoise. Lucky shouts, "Howdy!"

"Who are you?" asks Star Squirrel.

"Who am I? It's me—Lucky, your friend!"

"You cannot, cannot, cannot be Lucky," croaks Duke of Cannot.

"You are pink. We don't have pink friends. No pink friends for us. Our friend Lucky has beautiful white fur," honks Feather Goose.

"Yes, no, no, no pink friends for us," says Duke of Cannot.

Just then, a great big noise comes from down the path *Rummmmmmm, rummmmmmmm, rummmmmmmm!!! Screech!*

Scared by the unfamiliar sounds, the friends scatter into the forest to hide. Carefully, they watch.

"This looks like a grand place to live. Let's take it!" exclaims a young beaver.

Rummaging through her Roving Red Roadster, the mother beaver pulls out her "Lodge Sweet Lodge" sign and says, "We have found our new home."

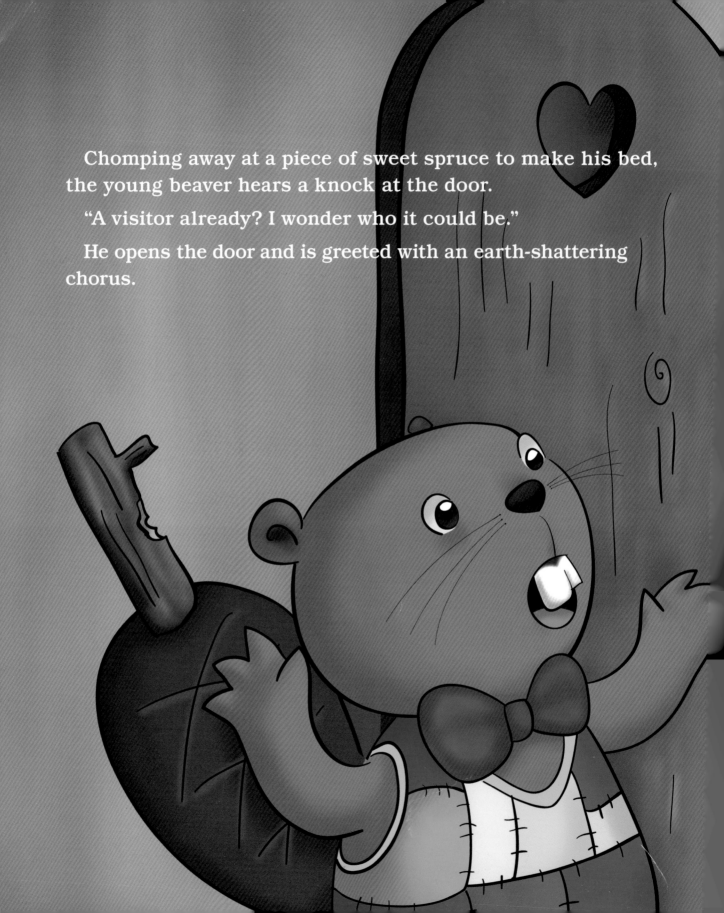

Chomping away at a piece of sweet spruce to make his bed, the young beaver hears a knock at the door.

"A visitor already? I wonder who it could be."

He opens the door and is greeted with an earth-shattering chorus.

Startled by the loud greeting, the young beaver jumps up.
"Don't be startled, dear. These are our new friends. Welcome to
our home!" declares the mother beaver. "What are your names?"

"I'm Star Squirrel!"   "I am Feather Goose."

"Allow me to introduce myself. I am Duke of Cannot."

"Who, who me? Are you asking me?" stutters Speedy Tortoise. "Oh, I'm ahhh... I'm ahh... well, I'm Speedy Tortoise. Yes, that's who I am. Yep, that's definitely me, Speedy Tortoise!"

"Oh, dear me, me, me. There he goes again," interrupts Duke of Cannot.

"Yeah, enough already!" says Feather Goose, rather angrily.

"Hello, hello to all of you!" shouts the young beaver.

"Well, what's your name?" Star Squirrel asks the young beaver.

"Why, I'm Patches, of course!"

"Patches?" inquires Speedy Tortoise.

"Patches? What kind of name is that?" exclaims Duke of Cannot. "I cannot, cannot, cannot remember ever hearing a name like that before. No, I cannot, cannot, cannot!"

"Why don't you share the story with your new friends?" the mother beaver asks Patches.

"Well, before I was born," answers Patches, "Momma was a great traveler and on these great travels she collected bits of fabric from all the wonderful places she visited..."

"Why would she do that?" interrupts Feather Goose.

"Yes, indeed. Why, why, why would anyone do that?" repeats Duke of Cannot.

"Allow me to explain," says Patches' Mother. "I made many treasured friends all over the world and was given beautiful fabrics like wool from Peru, cotton from Tunisia, embroidered fabrics from Ukraine, and silk from India. When I returned home, I kept these bits of fabric to remind me of the many friends and adventures we shared."

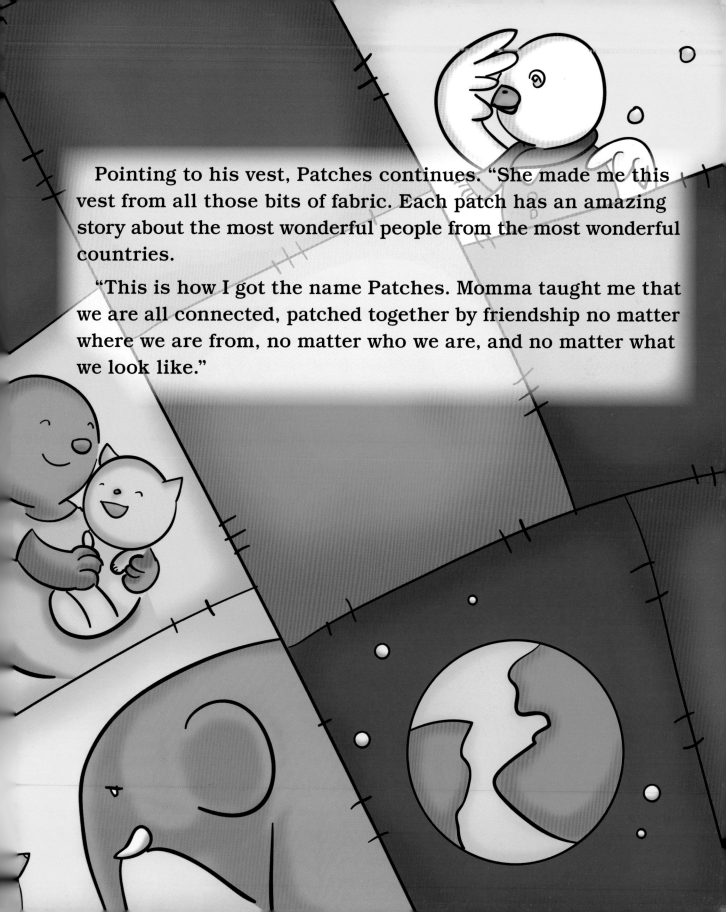

Pointing to his vest, Patches continues. "She made me this vest from all those bits of fabric. Each patch has an amazing story about the most wonderful people from the most wonderful countries.

"This is how I got the name Patches. Momma taught me that we are all connected, patched together by friendship no matter where we are from, no matter who we are, and no matter what we look like."

"What a wonderful story!" declares Star Squirrel.

"And what wonderful friends we can all be, too!" adds Patches.

"Well, what on earth are we waiting for?" says Speedy Tortoise.

Lodge Sweet Lodge ♡

"We must have a picnic to celebrate our new friendship with Patches!"

"Yes, a picnic. A picnic would be good, good, good," murmurs Duke of Cannot.

"A picnic at Reunion Bridge!" screams Star Squirrel.

Smiling with thoughts of his new friends and the celebration to come, Patches gathers his things and they all head out.

As they approach Reunion Bridge, the dark cloud that had been hovering on the horizon has gotten a lot closer.

"Oh, I do think the rain may ruin our picnic!" says Feather Goose.

"Rain? Did somebody say rain? Did it rain?" asks a rather confused Speedy Tortoise.

"Do you hear someone crying?" asks Patches.

Spotting a figure from behind the tree, Patches moves a branch aside.

"Well, what do we have here?" asks Patches. "Hello, I'm Patches the Beaver," he says, reaching out his hand to Lucky.

"Won't you shake my hand?"

"Not today, thank you," says Lucky sadly.

"Why are you so blue?" inquires Patches.

"Blue? I am not blue. I'm pink! Completely pink," cries Lucky.

"Pink as bubblegum!" Patches chuckles. "Pink is a beautiful color! Don't you think?"

"No, I don't think pink is a beautiful color, not if your friends don't recognize you, and don't want anything to do with you!" sobs Lucky as he looks at Feather Goose, Star Squirrel, Duke of Cannot, and Speedy Tortoise. "I'm Lucky. They have known me my whole life. We have been friends forever and now that I am pink as bubblegum, they abandon me. What am I going to do?"

The dark cloud moves directly over Lucky's head.

"Do? Why, you don't have to do anything. You just be yourself. That's what makes you Lucky, my new friend!" explains Patches.

"Patches is right, I suppose. Yes, yes, yes," states Duke of Cannot. "I cannot, cannot, cannot find a reasonable reason not, not, not to be your friend."

"But... but, he's pink!" stammers Feather Goose.

"Hmmm... I wonder?" questions Speedy Tortoise. "Could it be our Lucky after all?"

Feather Goose ponders for a moment and then says, rather decidedly, "I guess pink is a perfectly fine color. I don't have any pink friends. I think I might like a pink friend."

Lucky smiles, as the sweet words of his friends make his heart sing.

"It's like Momma always says," chuckles Patches, "a true friend is life's greatest gift."

The dark cloud finally begins to release its rain and, as it falls, cascading down Lucky's head, the pink begins to fade, slowly revealing his brilliant, soft and fluffy coat of fur.

The friends sit and watch in amazement as their old friend reappears.

"Lucky, it really is you after all!" cries Star Squirrel.

"You must come and join us for a picnic to celebrate our new friend Patches!" chimes Feather Goose.

"We brought your... we brought your... what did we bring?" asks Speedy Tortoise. "Oh, yes, we brought your favorite carrot soup, crisp lily pad salad, and ah, ah... oh yes, I remember... beet juice!" adds Speedy Tortoise.

"Oh, goody," shouts Lucky. "Who could ever get enough carrot soup, crisp lily pad salad, and beet juice!"

Raising his glass of beet juice to his new friends, Patches exclaims, "Here's to our future adventures!"